To Jamie. W. Barnsby

Christmas 2017.

Love from

Nanny xxx

Big Book of Aesop's Fables

Miles Kelly

First published in 2016 by Miles Kelly Publishing Ltd
Harding's Barn, Bardfield End Green, Thaxted, Essex, CM6 3PX, UK

Copyright © Miles Kelly Publishing Ltd 2016

This edition printed 2017

2 4 6 8 10 9 7 5 3 1

Publishing Director Belinda Gallagher
Creative Director Jo Cowan
Editorial Director Rosie Neave
Senior Editors Amy Johnson, Sarah Parkin, Claire Philip
Design Managers Joe Jones, Simon Lee
Senior Designer Rob Hale
Cover Designer Joe Jones
Production Elizabeth Collins, Caroline Kelly
Reprographics Stephan Davis, Jennifer Cozens, Thom Allaway
Assets Lorraine King

ISBN 978-1-78617-357-7

Printed in China

British Library Cataloguing-in-Publication Data
A catalogue record for this book is available from the British Library

ACKNOWLEDGEMENTS
The publishers would like to thank the following artists who have contributed to this book:
Advocate Art: Kate Daubney (The Boy who Cried Wolf), Monika Filipina (The Hare and the Tortoise),
Andy Rowland (The Town Mouse and the Country Mouse) and Barbara Vagnozzi (The Ant and the Grasshopper)

Made with paper from a sustainable forest

www.mileskelly.net

The Hare and the Tortoise

The hare was always boasting about how fast he could run. "I'm the fastest animal in the land," he would say.

One day the hare asked, "Who will run a race against me?"

The other animals were fed up with the hare's boasting, but no one would accept his challenge for fear of losing...

...no one except the tortoise.

5

"Ha ha!"

The hare laughed out loud. The other animals gasped.

The tortoise just smiled.

6

Preparations for the race began. The fox drew up a map of the route. The race was to take place the following week.

Whoosh!

For the next seven days the hare showed off, speeding around the meadow, dashing up hills, knocking animals over and upsetting just about everyone.

8

The tortoise just watched from afar as he chewed leisurely on grass and leaves.

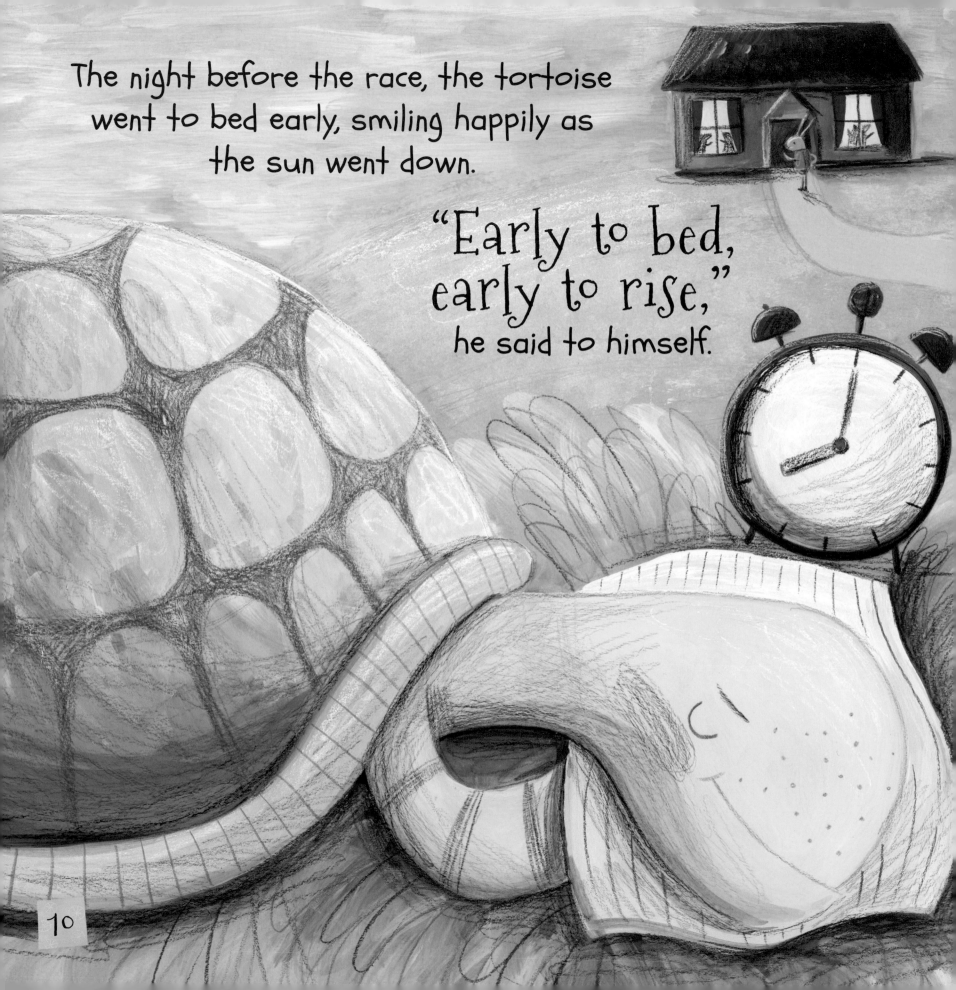

The night before the race, the tortoise went to bed early, smiling happily as the sun went down.

"Early to bed, early to rise," he said to himself.

10

SHHH!

Their noisy
antics kept
everyone awake.

Meanwhile, the hare stayed
up late, partying with his
neighbours, the badgers.

11

The next day dawned **bright and sunny.**

The tortoise awoke refreshed and full of energy. He ate a hearty breakfast then got ready for the race.

The hare wasn't feeling quite so refreshed. His late night meant he had hardly slept at all. He felt **exhausted.**

He poured himself a large glass of carrot juice and yawned loudly.

13

Out in the meadow, the animals were gathering for the race.

START

14

There were stalls selling cakes and sandwiches. Balloons and bunting had been tied to trees.

A party atmosphere was building!

At last it was time
for the race to start.

Feeling more like his usual
self, the hare took his place
at the start line.
"Get ready to lose!"
he said to the tortoise.

The tortoise just smiled. He didn't seem in the least bit worried.

Then the fox began the countdown to the race.

"On your marks... Get set..."
The whistle blew, and they were off!

17

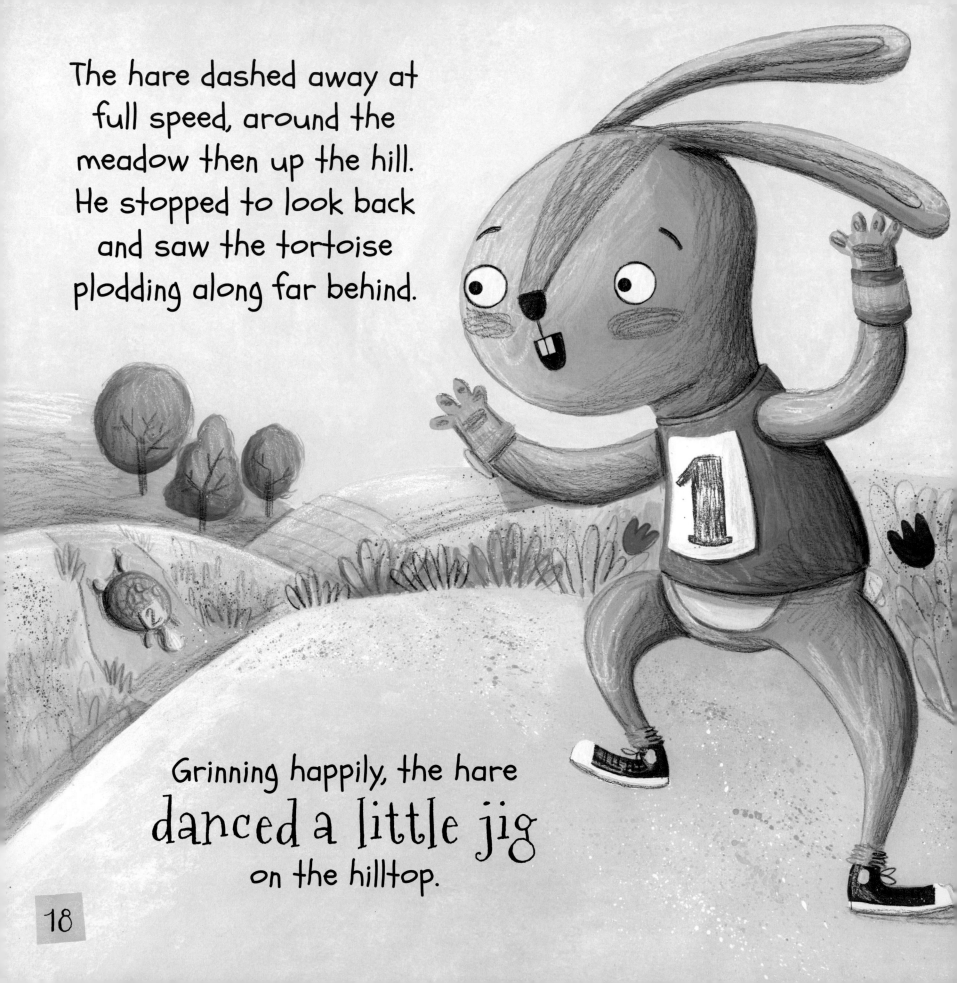

The hare dashed away at full speed, around the meadow then up the hill. He stopped to look back and saw the tortoise plodding along far behind.

Grinning happily, the hare danced a little jig on the hilltop.

18

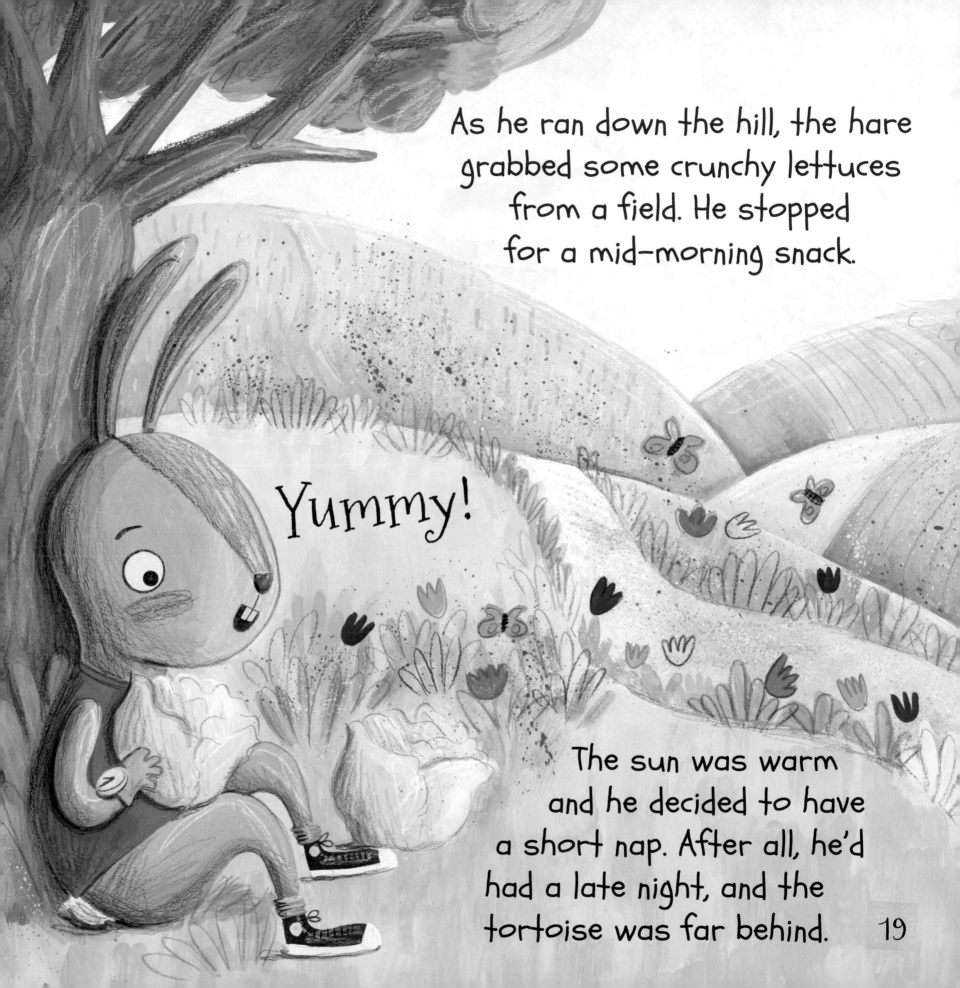

As he ran down the hill, the hare grabbed some crunchy lettuces from a field. He stopped for a mid-morning snack.

Yummy!

The sun was warm and he decided to have a short nap. After all, he'd had a late night, and the tortoise was far behind.

19

In the meantime, the tortoise carried on, up the hill and over the top.

ZZZZZ

He saw the hare snoozing
under a tree, and marched
bravely past.

The hare didn't stir a whisker.

21

Much, much later, feeling stiff and cold, the hare woke up with a start.

He looked up at the sun and saw how low it was in the sky. It must be almost evening! He feared the worst.

22

Pant!

Wheeze!

The hare flew around the rest of the route at top speed. He ran like he'd never run before.

But in the distance he heard shouting and clapping, and could just make out the tortoise nearing the finish line.

23

With the finish line in sight and the crowd roaring him on, the tortoise staggered on as fast as he could.

24

A few minutes later he crossed the line to huge applause and the crowd shouting his name.

25

The hare had lost his own challenge.

From now on perhaps he wouldn't be so boastful.

Slow and steady wins the race.

26

The Boy who Cried Wolf

There was once a shepherd boy called George, who tended his sheep on the hilly slopes just outside of his town.

Baa baa!

28

Baa baa!

He worked all day by himself and often got lonely and bored with just his flock for company.

29

George tried to find ways to keep himself busy.

He got the sheep to jump over a stile, and counted them one by one, but this just made him sleepy.

30

He even gave them funny hairstyles. But the sheep weren't impressed.

Baa!

Each morning George would move the sheep from field to field so that they could graze on the green grass.

But it was boring to watch them eat all day long.

32

He was fed up of having to rescue the silly sheep from hedges and ditches.

So one day, after spending all
morning trying to catch a naughty ewe,
George came up with an idea.

He left his flock
unattended and rushed
down the slopes towards
the town as fast as his
legs could carry him.

The townspeople jumped up and ran with George back to his flock.

They soon realized, however, that there was no wolf and returned to the town, grumbling.

George went back
to his duties for
the next few days,
but the weather
was cold and wet.

38

He didn't enjoy being out in the rain at all, and started to think about trying his trick again.

"You must come
and help me rescue
the sheep, otherwise
I will lose my flock!"

41

Again the townspeople came rushing to help him. But when they saw there was no wolf, just like the first time, they were very cross.

42

Soon after they left
George noticed something
moving in the trees.

He thought it was his eyes
playing tricks but then he
saw a furry body, bright
eyes and sharp teeth.

43

The wolf came rushing towards the sheep! They ran away as fast as they could!

44

George waved his arms and shouted at the wolf to leave – but it was no good!

So he turned and ran, crying "Wolf!" in earnest this time.

45

He rushed into the town calling for help, but no one would listen!

He ran to the butcher, who shook his head and said, "You've lied one too many times."

46

Then he ran to the baker, but he shook his head and sent him away.

Eventually George gave up and hurried back to his flock.

Some of the sheep were missing and the rest had scattered far and wide.

The wolf was fast asleep, looking fatter than before.

George shouted at the wolf to wake him and chased him away at last.

49

It took George all day
and all night to gather
the rest of his flock.

George had learnt that...

a liar will not be
believed, even when
he speaks the truth.

The Ant and the Grasshopper

It was a warm, sunny summer's day. There was a grasshopper in a field, and he was hopping about, chirping and singing very loudly.

Every day he sang, danced, played music and ate to his heart's content.

53

After a morning of singing and dancing,
the grasshopper started to feel tired.
He lay back on a leaf, dozing in the sun.

Huff!
Puff!

On the ground, just beneath the sleeping grasshopper, an ant was **hard at work.**

The ant's huffing and puffing awoke the grasshopper, who looked down from his comfy resting place to see what the noise was.

"Why are you working so hard? You should be resting and enjoying yourself, like me!" the grasshopper said to the ant.

"I have to work hard. I need to get all of my food stored and my nest ready for winter," the ant replied.

57

"But winter isn't for months," the grasshopper said. "Come and play with me."

"I don't have time for playing," the ant said. "I have too much to do. You should start collecting food and preparing your home for winter."

"I don't want to WORK or be inside on a beautiful day like this!" replied the grasshopper.

So the grasshopper kept playing. He sang songs and danced in the field.

Munch! Munch!

He slept in the sun and ate lots of food.

The ant continued to work, storing food and making his nest warm and cosy for winter.

In no time at all, the sun disappeared
and the weather turned cold. The
field became covered in a layer of
frosty white snow.

62

Winter had arrived!

Brrrr!

Crackle!

The ant was prepared for winter. While the snowflakes fell outside, the fire crackled inside his little nest.

He had enough food to see him through the cold months ahead.

65

The grasshopper searched for food, but he could not find any. He was very hungry.

And he had no shelter from the falling snow and bitter winds.

The grasshopper remembered the ant he had met in the summer. He **knocked** on his door and asked him if he had any **spare food**.

"Why don't you have any food of your own?" asked the ant. "Did you not store any in the summer? What were you doing?"

"I was so busy dancing and singing and eating that I didn't do any work at all!" said the grasshopper.

The grasshopper looked truly sorry and ashamed. He promised the ant he would work hard next summer and store his own food.

So the ant gave him as much food as he could spare.

It was just enough to see the grasshopper through the winter, but it was a miserable few months for him.

Next summer, the grasshopper was as good as his word. He worked hard to store enough food for himself.

The grasshopper
even found time to help
the ant, to make up for
his bad behaviour and
thank him.

73

So next winter the grasshopper didn't go hungry. He had learned his lesson, and now WOrkEd as well as Played.

There is a time for work and a time for play.

The Town Mouse and the Country Mouse

75

A little mouse who lived in a **busy, bustling town** was on a train to the country. He was going to visit his cousin. The town mouse was excited, as he had never been to the **country** before.

Meanwhile, the country mouse was hard at work preparing for the town mouse's visit.

After a long journey, the town mouse arrived. The cousins greeted each other joyfully.

"Hello!"

The country mouse showed off her home in a tree trunk. It was simple, but warm and cosy. "It doesn't look much like my home," the town mouse said.

Once the town mouse had rested, the country mouse took him to meet the farm animals next door. They crowded round to greet him.

Curious, the horse lowered his head and sniffed at the town mouse. "Watch it!" he cried. He wasn't keen on these new animals.

81

That evening, the country mouse
served a dinner of bread and cheese.
It was not at all like the fancy meals
the town mouse was used to.

All night, the town mouse tossed and turned in his bed of leaves.

He was used to sleeping in a much softer bed.

"How do you put up with this?" the town mouse asked in the morning. "Your food is plain and you sleep on leaves!"

84

"Come to the town with me and I'll show you how to live."

The country mouse was eager to see the town, so she agreed.

The town mouse lived
in a grand house in
the middle of town.
The country mouse
was amazed.

Inside, the town mouse proudly showed off his home. It was very **comfortable**.

87

The town mouse began a tour of the house. In the kitchen, they spotted a cat prowling around.

"Hide!" the town mouse whispered.

"Shhhhh!"

They scurried under a cup. Here they waited, hardly daring to breathe.

At last, the cat stalked away. "That was close!" exclaimed the country mouse, trembling.

89

They then went to the dining room.
On the table, they found a

delicious-looking feast.

There were sandwiches and pies, cakes and biscuits – everything that was good to eat. The mice helped themselves.

"I've never had food like this before!" mumbled the country mouse. The town mouse laughed. "This is how you could eat all the time!" he replied.

"Yummy!"

Suddenly, the mice heard growling and scratching at the door.

Two dogs burst in, sniffing the air.

93

The dogs began to
bark, jumping up
at the table.

94

The mice scampered away in fear.

95

Enough was enough.
The country mouse said goodbye
and left the town at once.

"Goodbye!"

"Better to live
poorly in peace
than richly in fear,"
she said.